This book is dedicated to my favorite animal in the whole world: the rabbit.

For Mom, Dad, and Kathryn, for Lauren, for Sean—
who steered me and cheered me and carried me on.
—H.B.

Some of the rabbits in this book were inspired by real rabbits from Red Door Animal Shelter in Chicago. If you enjoy this book, please consider donating to them at reddoorshelter.org or supporting your local animal shelter or rabbit rescue.

Carolrhoda Books®
An imprint of Lerner Publishing Group, Inc.
241 First Avenue North
Minneapolis, MN 55401 USA

For reading levels and more information, look up this title at www.lernerbooks.com.

Designed by Danielle Carnito.
Main body text set in Mikado medium and Century Schoolbook Std bold.
Typeface provided by HVD Fonts and Monotype Typography.
The illustrations in this book were painted with acrylics, black ink brush pens, and liquid gold leaf.

Library of Congress Cataloging-in-Publication Data

Names: Batsel, Hannah, author illustrator.
Title: A is for another rabbit / Hannah Batsel.
Description: Minneapolis : Carolrhoda Books, [2020] | Summary: Over the protests of Owl, a narrator introduces an alphabet consisting entirely of rabbits.
Identifiers: LCCN 2019016854 (print) | LCCN 2019019423 (ebook) | ISBN 9781541582200 (eb pdf) | ISBN 9781541529502 (lb : alk. paper)
Subjects: | CYAC: Rabbits—Fiction. | Alphabet—Fiction. | Owls—Fiction. | Humorous stories.
Classification: LCC PZ7.1.B3775 (ebook) | LCC PZ7.1.B3775 Aae 2020 (print) | DDC [E]—dc23

LC record available at https://lccn.loc.gov/2019016854

Manufactured in the United States of America
1-44821-35709-9/27/2019

A Is for Another Rabbit

HANNAH BATSEL

Carolrhoda Books
Minneapolis

B is for Bunny.

E is for Elephant.

Finally, this can become a proper, respectable alphabet book. I . . . wait a minute. There's something strange about that elephant . . .

F is for Fine, you caught me.
That wasn't an elephant.
And neither are these feisty,
fantastic, fluffy-tailed rabbits!

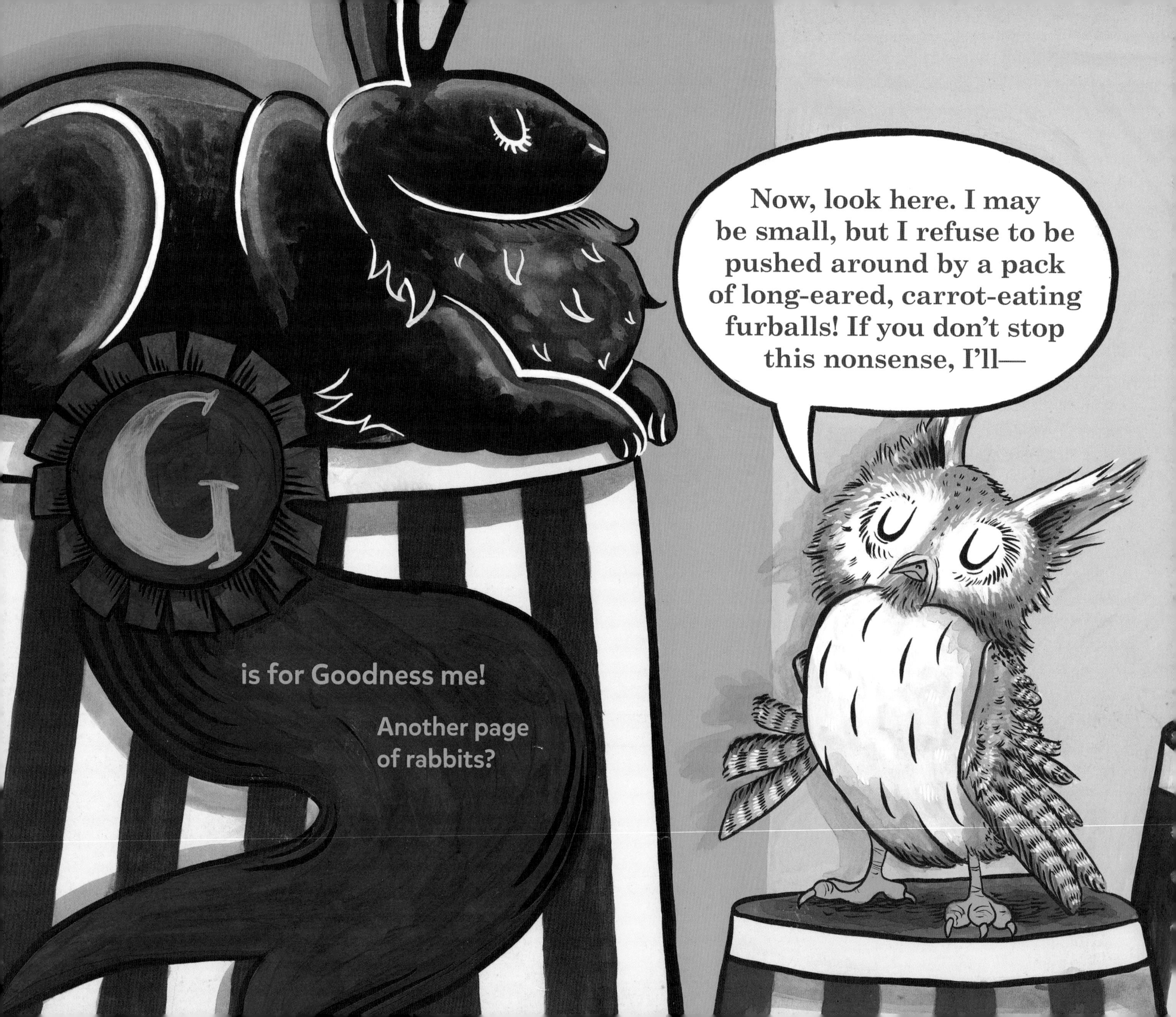

is for Goodness me!

Another page of rabbits?

H is for Hare.

Hares look similar to rabbits but are larger, wilder, and have even longer ears!

is for I've never seen such a gorgeous rabbit!

Look at that beautiful coat of fur!

J is for Just another rabbit.

Nothing to see here.

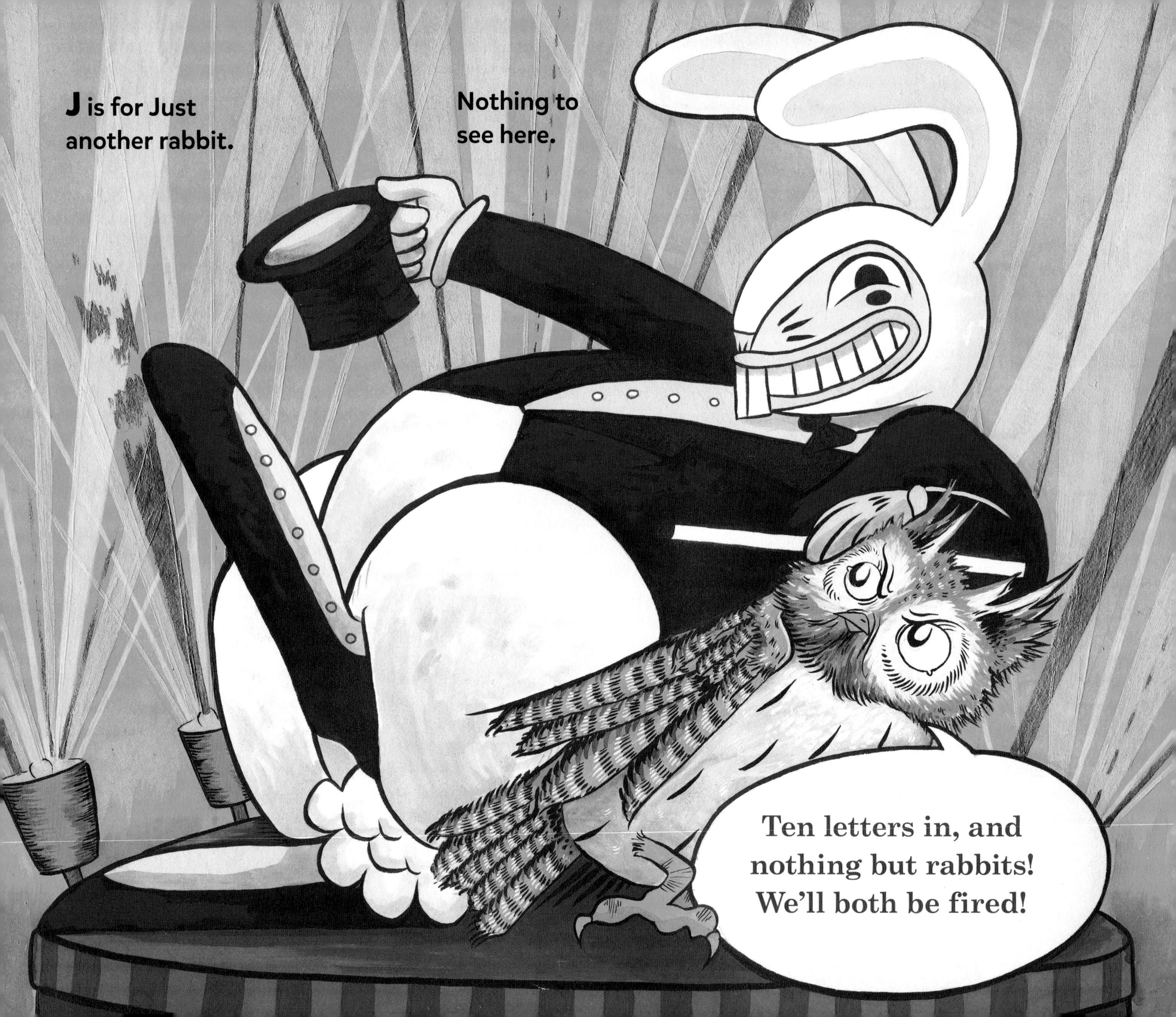

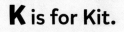

K is for Kit.

Hmm, "kite," eh? Well, that doesn't look like an animal to me, but at least you didn't say—

Not kite! Kit! "Kit" is the name for a baby rabbit.

L is for Long ears or short ears,
each rabbit's a prize.
A rabbit's a rabbit,
no matter the size!

Oh, are you a poet now? Here's a poem for you:

You've messed it up so much
I can't bear to look.
You and your rabbits
have ruined this book!

M is for My dear, dear friend. You seem a little tense.
Why don't you put on some slippers and rest for a moment?

Yes, I think that would be best. There's still time to rescue this book, after all.

N is for Nowhere near as many rabbits as I could have put on this page!

I wanted ten, but I've only drawn nine for your sake.
You're welcome.

O is for Oops! I didn't mean to disturb you. It's just difficult to control so many overzealous, obstreperous rabbits!

Where did you learn those words?

P is for Poor thing. All of this stress has gone to your head. I think you need a vacation, just for a couple pages. Why don't you let me take over?

Well, all right. Just for a few pages, though . . .

Q is for Quiet . . .

is he gone?

Yes, yes, yes!

I've been waiting for this next letter ever since we began.

Are you ready?

T is for Too late!

Tons and tons and tons of tiny, tenacious rabbits!

Up rabbits, down rabbits,
rabbits on swings!
Rabbits with roller skates,
rabbits with wings!

Very small rabbits
and tall rabbits too!
Artfully painted in
yellow and blue!

White rabbits, black rabbits, rabbits with spots!

Hop rabbits, lop rabbits, top rabbits, lots!

Young rabbits, old rabbits, every age! Rabbits on carousels!

Rabbits cavorting all over the place!

High-flying rabbits and rabbits in lace!

Rabbits onstage!

Zero on this page.

You've earned it. All clear.

But there sure are a whole
lot of rabbits right here!

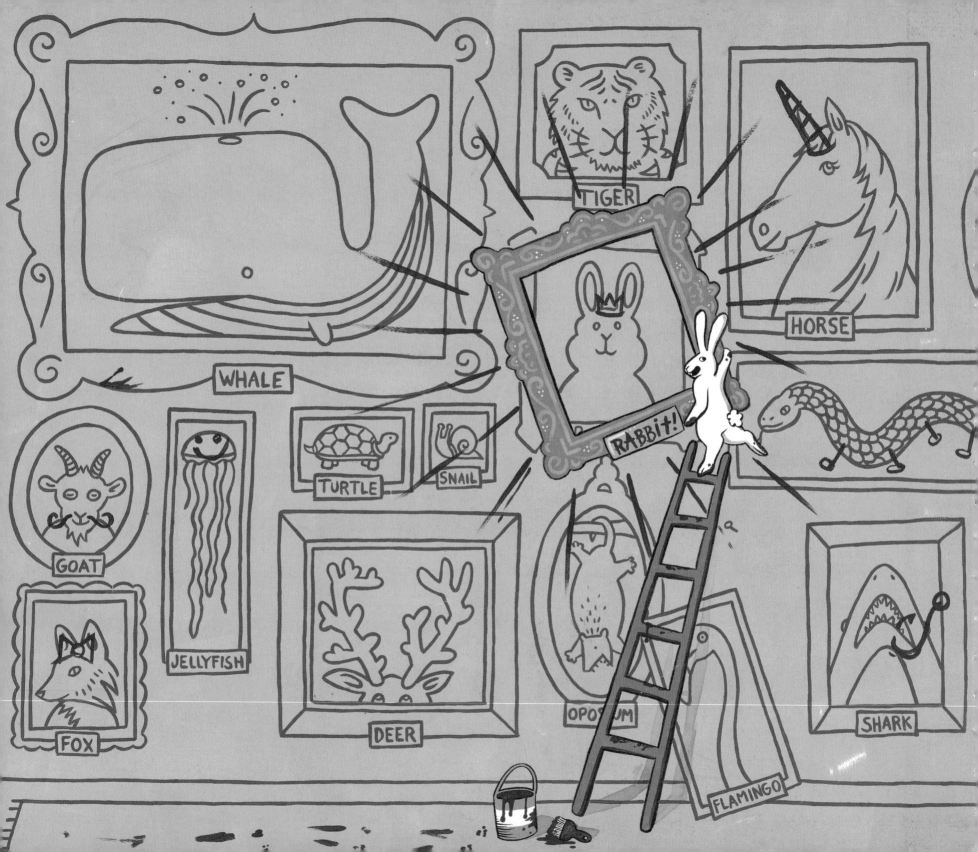